A STORY OF FAMILY AND FEAR

DEEP

AMY TEEGAN

DEEP

A Story of Family and Fear

AMY TEEGAN

Contents

Chapter 1

I don't want to be a father.

Ever.

And because of that choice, my wife has not spoken to me in over two weeks. Sixteen days, to be exact. The last thing she said to me was, "I can't help you, Will." And that was after another two weeks of barely acknowledging me whenever we were both in the house at the same time.

She's angry. I get that. But I don't know that I can do anything about it. I'm not going to change my mind, and it doesn't seem as though she will either.

I want to be fair to Robyn. She does, technically, have a right to be furious, given that I have been lying to her about this one thing since we met. I've known that I don't want kids for years, but I've deflected and avoided the conversation, choosing instead to let Robyn think that we're on the same page about that. I let her believe something that I knew was untrue.

But in my defense, I didn't tell her because—

No, wait. That would have been another lie.

I'm tired of lying.

Here's the truth:

I have felt broken since I was eight years old, and keeping this one thing, the reason I don't want kids, from my wife was a way of pretending I wasn't broken. By not telling her about it, I was able to go months—years, at times—without thinking about this deep wound in me. I was able to pretend I am just as normal as everybody else.

Not wanting kids is a symptom of what is truly wrong, what I've really been hiding.

But, also, I've been afraid that, if she were to learn the truth, if she were to finally see this thing that's wrong with me, she would not want to deal with it. That I would lose her altogether. I have been so afraid of losing her because of one thing that I let myself forget I could lose her for something else entirely.

So I've kept it a secret, this thing from my past that seems like it should be small, that sounds like it should not be such a big deal, but in reality has been a deep fissure around which I have made decades' worth of choices.

Despite my careful avoidance, almost a month ago, through a series of moments I suppose I should tell you about, Robyn found out I had been lying to her. She found out what I had been lying about. Her anger and hurt was such that she has said only a handful of sentences to me in the last month. It began strained and only grew worse with time, and since she last spoke to me we've lived side by side for two weeks without contact; she barely meets my eyes.

But this morning, when she left for work, I noticed that she had packed her overnight bag too. Though

Robyn did not actually tell me what she was doing or where she was going, the meaning was clear. The silence alone is not enough for her.

She's trying to get as far away from me as she can.

Robyn and I have been together for six years, married for just over four. We've been through a lot in that time, and I had fooled myself for so long, building my life without this big factor. I truly thought we had been honest with each other about all the baggage, big and little, that we were bringing to the relationship, since I had been so thoroughly able to block out the reality. We've made accommodations for each other; we've talked long into the night, reassuring each other. I've held her when she cried and she's cheered me up when I was feeling morbsy.

We've been a strong team through the good and the bad for more than half a decade. I thought nothing could shake us.

It's clear, though, that this is bigger than either of us was ready for.

I'm trying to see it from her point of view. The deception about our future aside, I know my fear isn't logical; it's silly, even. I know this; she knows this. So why am I letting it affect so much of my life? *Our* life? So much of what could lie ahead for us?

I think that's what is truly bothering her: that I've made a decision for both of us. Up until this, in everything else we have been partners, in the true sense of the word; I can't imagine how difficult this sudden change must be for her. Especially knowing that I have been keeping it from her for so long.

I know: I keep talking around it. Even all these years later it is difficult for me to look the thing in the eye.

Focusing on the problems in my marriage seems far easier.

Here's another truth:

I haven't taken a shower in twenty-four days.

Even so . . . that doesn't mean she should stop speaking to me. Sixteen days she has gone without saying a word to her spouse, her life partner, only communicating the bare minimum with a facial expression or by leaving a piece of mail out for me to find. Sixteen days without touching me. Sixteen days without being the support her husband needs right now.

It's not because I haven't showered. It's not even because I lied. It goes so much deeper than that.

It's because I am so absolutely petrified of passing on my fear of swimming to another generation that I refuse to have children at all, ever, biological or otherwise.

Sixteen days ago, I was in the master bathroom at my spot in front of our double sink. I was supposed to be at work in just under an hour and was washing up as best I could. The sink in front of me was half full of fairly hot water, and I stood in just my boxers in front of the mirror, soapy washcloth in hand to scrub my armpits.

But I was having trouble with the first step.

I could see the bottom of the sink easily. I wasn't even going to put my head under, and even if I was, this distress was stupid. I knew all the objections, all the logic, all the reasons my fears were patently absurd. I had talked myself through every step more than once; I had washed up this way for the entire week leading up to that. But you can't really reason with your subconscious. That amygdala really runs the show sometimes.

I took a deep breath, dipped the washcloth into the

water and out again, and stood there, slowly letting out my breath while I rubbed the bar of soap into the worn yellow terrycloth. I even closed my eyes—briefly—to hide the sight of the water.

Robyn, brushing her teeth in front of her own sink, watched me out of the corner of her eye.

The first day I skipped a shower, a week earlier, I told her why. Kind of. I must have underplayed it. It seemed like she didn't completely understand what was happening. The third day was when I started to be self-conscious about my smell. On top of all the other stress I was putting my wife through, having to suffer through body odor should not be part of it. I got the idea to just wash up in the sink. Using a washcloth instead of submerging any part of my body made a big difference (though I admit to still fighting down my anxiety). Leaning into the faucet to wet my hair was the worst part, but, I reasoned, it could be over quickly, and my feet never left the ground. Rinsing the suds from my hair was harder; I had even thought about shaving my hair completely off to make it easier to feel clean without dunking my head.

That morning—sixteen days ago, after a week of this—I had already turned the shower on and off twice in my attempts to overcome my terror, but it was no use. There wasn't time for me to argue with myself; I had to get to work. The compromise was washing up by hand over the sink. It's what I had been doing for nearly a week, so I'm not sure what it was about this particular day that made it tougher for me to get through, that so irritated Robyn.

"Will, just . . ." She took a sip of water, swished it around her mouth, and spit. "Explain it to me one more time. How is what you're doing all that different from stepping into the shower?"

I looked at her in the mirror, opened my mouth to retort, paused. This wasn't the first time she had asked me, though apparently however I was answering was not getting through to her or didn't make sense. I had lost count of how many times we'd had a version of this conversation.

"It's less water. And it doesn't go over my head. This feels manageable somehow."

"You could take a quick shower, though. In and out really fast, with just as little water. This just doesn't make any sense."

"I'm sorry. I don't know how else to explain it. I can't handle my head being under the water."

She sighed, frustrated, and leaned with her hip against the counter and arms crossed tight against her chest. "Fine. Okay. Whatever. For the sake of argument then, let's say you spend the rest of your life just washing your body in the sink. I still don't see what that has to do with whether or not we become parents."

"It's all connected, Rob. It's all part of the same thing, and . . . I wouldn't feel right. I would fuck up our kids, and I'd regret it the rest of my life."

"That's such bullshit, Will. And, frankly, incredibly narcissistic. Everyone has issues in their childhood, everyone learns how to deal with them. Think about how many awful people are just pumping out kids with no thought. You're a coward."

"Yes!" I said, seizing onto that word. Maybe I had finally made my point. I turned from the sink to face her.

"I am afraid, and I am not brave enough to fight through it. Maybe it's self-centered, but . . ."

What I left unsaid was that I was fine being self-centered if it kept some poor, innocent child safe. What I left unsaid was that calling me a coward was not going to make me change my mind.

She stared at me, her mouth open, for a good five seconds before choking back a laugh. Or a sob. I'm not sure which.

"Are you serious?"

I nodded.

"There's nothing I can do to change your mind?"

I shook my head.

"For fuckssake," she whispered.

"I'm working on it."

"Are you?" She took a deep breath. "I can't help you, Will."

Then she leaned toward the mirror again, wordlessly applied her lipstick, and left the bathroom without another glance my way.

For the last sixteen days we have been living separate lives. She doesn't greet me when she gets home from work, nor wish me goodnight when she heads up to bed. She acts as though she is deaf to any question, comment, or offer I make—and I try multiple times each day.

I even tried walking back my assertion that we should not have kids. That we could maybe kind of think about talking about it sometime in the future. Back to the same deflection I've been using for years.

She's too smart to fall for it again. She stared hard at me, her expression a challenge, a look that said *coward* as she silently willed me to acknowledge all the ways I was letting her down.

I think the only thing that will really get through to her is if I take a shower. Prove I'm not afraid. That I'm working on facing my fears. That will be the big step that demonstrates to her I can change in my thinking.

Two days after Robyn stopped speaking to me, I knew I had to do something. This was on me. It didn't matter how understanding she could be if there were still things that I could do about it.

I work in a large accounting firm, the kind where most of our clients are medium-sized businesses with several people assigned to each team. I'm a forensic accountant, so most of my work hours are spent secluded in my tiny office as I dive deep into muddled spreadsheets from three years ago. The problem-solving and hyper-focus really appeal to me.

But it also means that I had a quiet, isolated corner in which to try to solve my marriage problems. Fifty-three hours after Robyn said her last words to me, I was carefully trawling the internet for a therapist (both appropriate to my problem and accepted by my insurance, not an easy combo). It took me most of my lunch hour, combing every review site I could find, but I narrowed it down to one woman, near my office building, in-network, who could fit me in the following week.

That meant another seven days at least of Robyn icing me out. Unless I could manage to fix this on my own. Which I had tried and failed to do already. Many times over the previous two-plus decades.

Still, I was proud of myself. After so long suffering through this fear, I was taking steps.

That night, when Robyn got home, I was in the kitchen chopping the carrots for the fried rice I was preparing. I heard her open the front door, hang up her coat, toe off her shoes, and walk lightly into the kitchen.

"Hey, babe," I said. "Dinner will be ready in forty minutes or so."

She looked at me deliberately, then looked away, again deliberately, and opened the fridge.

"I started a bottle of wine," I added, indicating the open white sitting on the island.

She reached far in the back of the fridge for a can of seltzer and turned her back on me.

The oven beeped, letting me know it had preheated, but I ignored it. I might not have another chance tonight. Before Robyn could get to the doorway of the kitchen and shut me out for the rest of the evening, I tried again.

"I made an appointment with a therapist."

Slowly, deliberately, Robyn turned back to face me. Tilting her head, she examined me from the other side of the room.

"I don't meet with her until Tuesday, but I hope that . . . I mean, maybe with this we can . . . you know?"

How many different ways can I ask my wife to speak to me?

"I'm trying, Robyn."

She offered me a half smile of polite disbelief before leaving again.

She had heard me. At least I knew she was listening and wasn't completely ignoring my existence. Though evidently it was not enough to warrant a response.

The days went by and still Robyn didn't speak to me. We were home together the entire weekend, but she made every effort to not be in the same room as me. She had started sleeping in the guest room a couple nights earlier, but now she didn't even eat the same food as I did. Saturday afternoon the doorbell rang, and I answered it to find a DoorDash guy handing over a single sub sandwich and a soda. I'd pulled out a roast to thaw, but my wife had given no hint that she was ordering food. When I turned away from the door, she was there to take her food from me and then disappear back into the guest room. I returned to the kitchen to turn off the oven.

At this point I got angry. What could she be doing? How could my trauma so bother her that she holed up alone for days on end? It seemed selfish to me; it seemed an overreaction. She was my wife. Shouldn't she be more supportive about what I was going through?

But whenever I thought of confronting her about it, I kept coming back to that last conversation, those last words.

"I can't help you, Will."

These last several years I'd thought I had been doing so well. I was sure I had put this behind me—I'd told my wife that I had before we married. I had told her there was nothing to worry about, that this fear came up occasionally, but it was nothing we couldn't handle together.

But in fact, here I am again, and each time I get triggered the experience is worse and worse. I might need to accept the fact that I may never be free of this.

I'm stuck here. It's too deep in me.

All because of Grandma Penny.

Chapter 2

Grandma Penny.

In many ways she was both the best and the worst part of my childhood.

When I was three years old and my little sister was almost one, my Grandma Penny came to live with my family in Ventura, California. My mom had just gotten a full-time job, her first since I was born, and Grandma Penny was going to look after us in lieu of my parents paying for childcare. I learned the details and timeline later, of course; I don't have any memories of my life before she was in it every single day.

My grandmother was an enormous woman. In my memory, she was as tall and as wide and as sturdy as a refrigerator. She had grown up on a farm in the Midwest, where such size and strength were assets, and she never seemed to be ashamed by it the way other women might be. When I tripped and hurt my knee, she'd scoop me up and carry me to the bathroom to wash the wound. Or later, when I went to school, I would come home to find she had rearranged the living room all by herself. Even when I'd grown to be some inches taller than her, I always had that nagging feeling that if she really tried, if she really wanted to, she could likely beat me at arm wrestling.

The first few years she lived with us, I all but worshipped her. For all I knew at that age, she was the one taking care of me—but, more to the point, she was the one playing with me. Every aspect of my life involved Grandma Penny. I wouldn't do anything without first checking to see if she wanted to do it with me. We built LEGOs together, and she watched me climb trees over and over again. During the times of the day when she was cooking or folding laundry, for example, I was right at her side, pretending to be keeping house too. She even sewed a tiny apron for me that matched hers, since she called me her little helper. (I bet my dad loved that.)

Though her actual first name was Dorothea, Grandma Penny was so named because she always had pennies in her pocket for me, and that fact was all I needed to differentiate her in my little three-year-old mind from my mother's mother, Grandma-who-lived-in-Florida. She carried the coins with her because she liked to play a game where she would "find" pennies in my pockets or in the part in my hair or under my armpit.

"Well, look at that. Billy is leaking pennies again," she would call to the house, finding yet another penny a few inches behind my foot that had allegedly fallen out of my pant leg. "They're just all over the floor."

My favorite part of her "finding" these pennies on me, of course, was that I always got to keep them. I'd store them in my pockets, accumulating a penny or two every day, and I loved the weight of them. When they got to be too full I'd empty my pockets into the ceramic dinosaur coin bank that I had painted at one of those paint-your-own-pottery places. I remember trying to stay awake as long as I could after I got tucked in at night, dreaming up all the things I could spend my pennies on. I had no idea what a superhero LEGO set could cost, but surely my bank full of all those pennies must come close.

I was born William; my parents called me Will and my sister—when she started to speak—called me "Wiwh," since she struggled with her *l*'s. Grandma Penny was the only one who called me Billy, and I adored her too much to ask her to do otherwise. She was also the only one who spoke to me as though I was a big kid, never speaking down to me, never limiting her vocabulary.

As soon as my parents were out the door for work, it was, "Billy, please pull the sheets off your bed for me," or, "Billy, tell me, do you think your mother would prefer eggplant parmigiana or lasagna for dinner?"

I had never heard of eggplant, let alone whatever that other fancy word was, but that didn't stop me from answering confidently, as though my mother's nuanced opinions on varieties of Italian dishes were my personal expertise.

"Lahz—lahzah . . ."

"Lasagna, huh?" she'd say, ignoring my embarrassment that I couldn't pronounce it. "I think you're right."

As my father's mother, Grandma Penny was immensely proud of how much I ate and how fast I grew. I heard over and over that I would grow up to be as tall as my father—six and a half feet tall—if I ate all the eggs and oatmeal she made every morning.

"This is what I fed your father for breakfast every single day, and look how he turned out. Big and strong, just like you will be, Billy."

I tried to clean my plate every meal; I really did. It was nearly always too much food for me, but I always tried. I wanted her to be proud of me. I wanted to grow up to be just like my father. She took such a personal pride those few times I managed to eat everything off my plate, but then it seemed like the next meal she would serve me an even bigger portion.

As far as I know, that was the only way I ever disappointed her. In every other aspect of my young life, Grandma Penny was my biggest fan, my loudest cheerleader, and my best friend. For two years, my whole life was Grandma Penny. My sister, Kayla, was around, I guess, but I don't remember much. She was so little and, at that age, napped a lot. All of my memories from then revolve around Grandma Penny.

But soon the day approached when I would need to leave my little bubble of love and family. I was born in the summer, so around my fifth birthday my parents and grandmother started preparing me for going to kindergarten.

"You're such a big kid now," my dad said, "you'll get to go every day to see the world and learn new things."

"You'll get to go make new friends," my mother said as she beamed at me.

Grandma Penny dished mashed potatoes onto my plate.

"But . . ." I looked around the table, confused. "But I

don't want to go anywhere. I want to stay here. Why are you sending me away?"

"Oh, honey, we're not sending you anywhere," Mom said. "It'll just be a few hours every day. You'll be back home in the afternoon."

I looked at Grandma Penny, silently pleading with her to tell me this was all a joke. That she didn't want me to leave either.

Instead, she brightened up and leaned toward me. "Billy, do you remember that big red-brick building we pass when we walk to get slushies sometimes? Do you remember what it is?"

I nodded.

"That's where you'll be. Close enough to home that if anything happens, I can be there right away."

"But what's going to happen?" I asked, my voice cracking.

"Nothing, buddy," my dad said, shooting his mother a look that I could not interpret. "I promise. We wouldn't make you do anything that could be bad for you. Just . . . trust Mom and Dad, okay?"

I nodded again, too upset to be able to put words to my fear.

When the first day of school finally arrived some weeks later, I was so scared. I kept hoping someone would tell me it was all a joke. However, after breakfast, when neither of my parents had left for work, when they wanted to take a photo of my outfit that day, as I wore my small red backpack, the whole situation felt more and more real. I learned they had both taken the morning to walk me to school. At the time, of course, I didn't understand why they would do that, why we would leave

Grandma Penny behind. It seemed so final and definitive to be walking between my parents, one hand in each of theirs, while they transported me to this completely unknown and undesired location.

It's surprisingly easy to separate out my memory of that very first day of school from memories of other days as a kid—I was more upset that day than I had ever been before. Each moment feels crystal clear, as though I'm watching a movie of it.

"You are going to have such a good day," my mother said, squatting next to me and straightening the collar of my jacket unnecessarily.

"We can't wait to hear all about it, buddy," my father said, placing his big hand on the top of my head and ruffling it—also unnecessarily. "We'll have a special dinner for you tonight, to celebrate your special day, and you can tell us everything."

"But why do I have to go? I don't want to. I want to go home," I pled with them, "with Grandma Penny. She said we would make cookies!"

"You can do that after school, Will," Dad said. "But first you get to have your very first day of kindergarten."

My teacher, sweet Mrs. Lansdale, stood watching in the doorway of her classroom. She had already been a kindergarten teacher for at least two decades when I had her, and she always spent her first morning attentive to all her little charges as they arrived, aware of any tears or terror that might be occurring. But to me, five years old and about to be abandoned by my entire family, she looked like a serpent slithering into my nightmares. She couldn't have been much older than early forties, but I imagined her a wrinkled, leathery dragon, hoarding her treasure—in this case small children, of whom I was one. My parents had stayed home from work in order to hand me over to this creature and then abandon me to her.

"We'll see you in a few hours, all right?" Mom said. She kissed my forehead and stood again.

I burst into tears.

"Will, honey, what's wrong? Aren't you excited about getting to go to school with all those kids your own age?"

But I could only bawl out, "Why are you leaving me?"

"Oh, baby . . ." My mom squatted next to me again. "It's just for a little while. Just a few hours. It'll be over before you know it, and then you will be so excited to come back tomorrow."

"I have to come back *tomorrow*?!" I wailed.

My dad sighed. "Buddy, come on. We talked about this."

"Why didn't Grandma Penny come?" I sobbed harder, barely able to get the words out of my mouth. "Is —is she m-m-mad at me?"

I didn't see it, but I imagine my parents exchanged some kind of look over my head. How could they reason with a distraught child who didn't even completely understand what he was upset about?

"Why don't you go with Mrs. Lansdale, buddy," my dad said, gesturing her over. "She knows all about the first day of school and will be here all day with you."

"What's your name?" my new teacher said gently, bending down to my eye level. "I'd love if you told me about the character on your T-shirt."

But I wouldn't be distracted. I refused to be comforted. In my mind, Grandma Penny would be so upset I had left her. I hoped that she wouldn't make cookies without me; it was always my job to roll the snickerdoodle dough in the sugar and cinnamon. As far as I knew, we had done virtually everything together up to that point in my life. How could I have gone away from home for so long without her?

As clear as my memory of my agitation before school is, I truly don't remember anything about what happened inside the classroom.

But even the terrible, dreaded things in life come to an end eventually.

As Mom and Dad had promised me, kindergarten was only a half day. Nowadays, as far as I understand, schools have elaborate systems in place to make sure that young children are not thrust unaccompanied into the world after school, but the late '80s were much more relaxed.

So, when my class was released just after noon that day, I pulled on my backpack—now heavier than when I had arrived that morning—and wandered out into the August sunshine. As my eyes adjusted to the afternoon brightness, I looked around hopelessly.

From the door of the kindergarten room I could see the small parking lot, where twenty or more adults stood chatting and waiting. Not a single one of them looked familiar to me, and I again felt that certainty that I had been abandoned. A couple of the girls from my class darted past me as they spotted their own grownups, and I felt myself shrinking back with my disappointment.

But then I noticed another grownup, crossing the street from the neighborhood next door, smiling at the crossing guard in her reflective vest. She wore the bright red polyester pants that matched her rose-covered blouse, and she carried my toddler sister in her arms. And she was looking right at me.

Grandma Penny had walked from home—likely delayed some by three-year-old Kayla's little legs—to meet me after my first day of school.

Once she had crossed the street, she kept walking toward me, across the grass, never once pausing or even looking away. She finally stopped, smiled, and held out her hand for me to take.

I burst into tears, sobbing so hard with relief that I almost couldn't walk the final few feet to get to her.

Chapter 3

Eventually I got used to kindergarten, as all kids do. And in time I even found myself looking forward to school, in part because of how much Grandma Penny seemed to love my stories when I got home. She was home with Kayla most of the time, and persisted in treating me like an intrepid adventurer, a conquering hero returning home victorious every afternoon. In those days, my grandmother was my best friend and I trusted her completely. Every day until the fall after I turned eight she was my stalwart and my foundation and my protector and everything.

But then, when I turned eight years old, she decided it would be a good idea to share a new hobby of hers with me, and everything changed.

I mentioned before that Grandma Penny always spoke to me as an adult. She treated me older than I actually was. She framed everything as my choice, allowing me to set my own boundaries and determine for myself what I was ready for. None of my friends had anything close to that kind of freedom. My grandmother continued this practice throughout my childhood as well as my sister's. Like when I started reading *Pet Sematary* at age ten and only got two pages in before I was uninterested (my friend Logan's mom was shocked when she overheard me saying I was reading it). Or when I begged to be taken to the museum with the dinosaur bones and was the only six-year-old trying to read the long, scientific plaques that stood by each exhibit.

Letting me decide what I was ready for worked almost every time.

(Until it didn't. I'm getting to that.)

One June weekend, just a couple weeks after I turned eight, our parents left Kayla and me with Grandma Penny for several days. They didn't leave all that often; I don't think we could really afford extravagant vacations. But in this case, it was my father's tenth high school reunion weekend, and it was important to them to go back to Idaho and see his friends.

Plus, wasn't this one of the reasons Grandma Penny lived with us anyway? Built-in childcare.

This particular weekend, my little sister was feeling sick. It was her third time getting a cold since the beginning of the year, so the family had more or less fallen into a routine around it. Kayla got to stay in Mom and Dad's bed all day and watch television in between napping. She had three VHS tapes of movies that she watched over and over and over. I practically had the movies memorized, and I didn't even watch them with her that often. I'd go check on her every hour or so, or Grandma Penny would, making sure Kayla had water or Kleenex, but she was more or less left to herself.

I remember that Friday after school, sitting on my bedroom floor hunched over my *LEGO City* train station set. Through my open door floated the sounds of Billy Joel singing about not worrying.

Grandma Penny appeared in the doorway, dust rag in hand. She took up most of the doorframe, and she looked at me expectantly.

"I thought, with your parents gone, it might be fun to have pizza for dinner."

My eyes lit up. "With sausage?"

"Of course! And pepperoni?"

"But no mushrooms."

She looked at me with mock horror. "Mushrooms? How could you even suspect such a thing of me?"

"Thank you, Grandma."

I turned my focus back to the toy, but she had more to say.

"And I also thought, maybe, since it's a special night with your parents gone and your sister sick, you might want to stay up late with me?"

"Really? How come?"

"Now that you're eight years old, I think you're grownup enough for me to show you something. Something that means a lot to me. If that's all right with you?"

I thought about how excited Grandma Penny had been when I showed her my new LEGO set, or when I told her about a special art project that we had done at school. I remember thinking that I didn't like to read the kinds of books she was always reading, books with shirtless men and pastel colors. In my eight-year-old self-centeredness, I had no idea how else she liked to spend her time. For all I knew she existed only to cook and clean for my family, praise me and give me attention, and nothing else.

But I nodded. Yes, of course. Of course, Grandma Penny, I want to spend time with you. Of course I want you all to myself while Kayla's asleep.

"Okay, Grandma. What is it?"

"I think I'll let that be a surprise. We'll have pepperoni and sausage pizza and I'll tell you all about it. All right, Billy?"

"Yes!"

"But there's something I want you to do for me first."

I nodded.

"Go play outside, my boy. You've been in here far too long. You still have thirty minutes before the pizza is here. Stretch your legs, and I'll call you when it's time for dinner."

I stifled my groan, not wanting to see her disappointed expression at how little time I spent outside. Thirty minutes would feel like an eternity when I was looking forward to pizza and thinking about my LEGOs. But I did as she asked, climbing the tree in our small backyard and pretending to be an astronaut in a rocket high above the earth. Somehow the time passed, and then I was that much hungrier when she finally called me back inside for the night.

"What is it you wanted to do tonight, Grandma?" I asked when I walked into the kitchen. I tried to play it cool, to be nonchalant about it, but inside I was excited at the millions of possibilities that soared through my mind.

She pulled two plates down out of the cupboard and set them on the counter next to the pizza box. "Well.

Now that you're such a big boy, I wonder if you might want to watch one of my favorite movies with me."

"Can we eat in the living room?"

"Absolutely. That's one of the best parts of movie night. You need to sit on the floor and eat at the coffee table, though."

"Okay. But I get to stay up late?"

I'm sure my eyes were big as saucers. I don't remember crossing the room to her; for all I know I floated over there, powered by the sheer strength of my excitement.

"It's a special movie." She handed me my plate with two slices and led me into the living room. As she placed a couple napkins and a cup of milk on the coffee table for me, she continued. "I rented this movie just for this weekend."

"You did?" I was in awe, settling down to my food. "Why is it special?"

"Oh, a lot of reasons. This movie is older than I am."

I didn't see how that was possible, but knew better than to say so.

"And it's well loved by many people. It was one of my favorites when I was your age, and, actually, I told my parents I wanted to be a movie star after I saw it."

"Were you?"

She chuckled. "Heavens, no. At that time movie stars had to be able to sing and dance, and I have two left feet."

I didn't know what that meant, but before I could ask she had gone to her purse, which was on the floor by the front door.

"Here it is."

From out of the depths of her gigantic bag she pulled

a VHS tape, plastic case and label stickers from the rental shop evident. From where I sat on the couch, I could only make out a big yellow title and four strangely dressed characters on the front of the case, before Grandma Penny was putting the tape in the player.

"We'll have to keep the volume down," she said. "We don't want to wake your sister. She's not quite big enough to see this, and if she wakes up we'll have to turn it off."

I nodded vigorously, determined to not make any more noise than I absolutely had to.

"All right, then." She smiled at me. Her bulk blocked all of the television screen when she turned back toward the couch. "You just stay put, little man. I'm going to get my pizza and I'll bring back some popcorn for us."

She left the room, but the tape had already started playing. The previews began, and in my film-starved youth, every one of them blew me away. I had been taken to see the *DuckTales* movie in the theater the previous summer, but every other movie I had asked to see I was rebuffed. My father insisted that I wasn't old enough to understand; my mother was worried I wouldn't be able to pay attention. Even Grandma Penny thought I'd be better off playing outside than staying in and watching a story. So the little bit of magic and promise in the movie previews was all new to me. And I was hooked.

By the time my grandmother returned—carrying a huge, warm, buttery bowl of popcorn—I had been introduced to three more movies, teased by the characters and the stories.

After the previews, the title cards of the movie started. Big, scrolly letters in kind of a sepia-toned landscape. It was a lot of words, and I couldn't read that fast, but

Grandma Penny told me that it was a list of all the men and women who had worked on the movie. But also that I didn't have to pay close attention to it yet.

That gave me time to eat my pizza. I practically inhaled it so I could focus all my attention on the movie when the story part started.

I had just wiped my greasy fingers on my napkin for the last time when the words faded. The sepia tone remained, and the first thing we saw was a teenage girl and a little dog running down a dirt road. They stopped and the girl talked, and I learned that they were being chased, and from that moment I could not look away.

I'm sure you can imagine my audible gasp when the movie turned to technicolor.

I was rapt until the very end, blowing past my usual bedtime (and completely disregarding my usual disdain for people singing if they're not playing instruments).

Almost two hours later, as soon as the end card filled the screen, I turned to Grandma Penny.

"Can we watch another one?"

That was the start of an intense love affair I had with classic movies. Every weekend Grandma Penny would rent at least one, and whenever my parents went out she would get two or three. We watched *You Can't Take It with You*, *The Secret Life of Walter Mitty*, and *Fantasia*. We reveled in *Meet Me in St. Louis* and *Singin' in the Rain*. We watched every one of her favorite movies and some of them became mine too. It didn't always work out. She was surprised that I didn't seem interested in *The Maltese Falcon* —"A heist movie, Billy!"—but never pushed anything on me that I didn't want to watch. We even tried *Mr. Smith Goes to Washington*, but as much as I grew up to love Jimmy

Stewart, there was just far too much paperwork and monologues in that movie to interest me at that age. That went on for months, and even today I can still recall some of the more iconic scenes. I don't remember much about *North by Northwest*, but that chase scene with the airplane is seared in my mind.

One night late in the fall, close to the holidays when my parents started having more dinner or party plans with friends, Grandma Penny brought home another tape from the rental store.

"Up for another old movie with your old grandma?" she asked over dinner.

Kayla was put to bed right after supper. By the time Grandma Penny came out to the living room and put the tape in the player, I had already made our microwave popcorn (the one thing I could "cook" by myself at that age) and was waiting on the couch for her.

"What are we watching tonight? Is it good?"

"I haven't seen it yet. I'm told it's about scientists and adventure. This one's almost as old as I am, but not quite. My friends tell me it's good and that their grandchildren love it. But it's new for me too. We can watch it for the first time together. There aren't many old movies we can say that about, you know."

"Wow," I breathed.

And with that, the movie began.

Chapter 4

Grandma Penny hit **PLAY** on the VHS player.

My parents were out with friends, Kayla had been put to bed, and I was once again allowed to stay up late on a Friday night watching an old movie with my grand-mother. She had rented something special, she said, and I didn't know what to expect. It might seem strange that an eight-year-old would so love movies made fifty years before he was born, but this had quickly become one of my favorite ways to spend my time. So when Grandma Penny said that she hadn't actually seen this movie yet, it didn't occur to me to worry. I trusted her completely and could not wait to see what she wanted me to see.

The old, original Universal International title card appeared, in black and white, the lettering over a model of a globe.

"This one was made a little later than the others. I was maybe twelve years old or so when it came out."

"But you haven't seen it?"

"No, I never did. My older brother snuck out of the house one night and watched it in the theater." She chuckled, adding, "He got in so much trouble."

"Really? How come?"

"Oh, who knows." She waved away my question. "My father was much more strict with me than your parents are with you. He got it into his head somehow that this would be too scary for my siblings and me."

I wondered if my parents knew about all the movies Grandma Penny let me watch. They knew about some of them—I had wanted to be the Cowardly Lion for Halloween—but maybe not all. Whenever we watched a movie that was potentially too mature for me, there was this thing Grandma Penny would do. If I ever asked a question about a character or the plot that could not be easily answered, she would purse her lips, look at the ceiling, and finally say, "Ask me again in about eight years."

Somehow those were never scenes or questions I brought up in front of my parents later.

This movie, this one Grandma Penny had not yet seen, began with a sinister tone. At the time I didn't think anything of it. Many of the other films had started similarly, after all.

"And you never saw it after you grew up? Not once?"

She shook her head. "Remember, Billy, it's only in the last few years that folks have had things like VHS players to watch movies when they wanted to. It's likely that this movie played on television, some late night or two, but never when I had a chance to watch it. I've been waiting several decades to see what all the fuss was about."

After the film company's logo, the ominous orchestration was all horns and crashing symbols that hinted at the kind of movie we were about to see. Huge, angular words forming the title appeared, gray on a dark sky background. Mysterious and striking and maybe even a little bit chilling.

While the scary music played over the title and opening credits, I looked at Grandma Penny. She was leaning forward expectantly, eyes wide and with a faint smile on her lips. I looked back to the screen where the opening credits were rolling. I could read, but not as fast as the movie went, so I spent the first minute or so watching my grandmother.

Since I grew up, these memories of Grandma Penny are all colored by what happened later. At the time, when I trusted her completely and was grateful for every movie she let me watch, I suppose I assumed she was excited to watch the story play out as much as I was. Now, though, I wonder how much of her interest in this movie was a belated teenage rebellion. A gift to her younger self that had been so sheltered and held back and insulated from the world. Surely, at fifty-plus years old, this woman had an inkling of an idea of what this movie was about and how it might not be appropriate for a young kid. Especially right before bedtime. I wish I'd asked her what she remembered about her brother seeing it, what objections her father might have had.

I was always—always—given the choice to stop a movie, to set aside a book, to say when I had changed my mind about something. At any point during the watching of this movie I could have asked to turn it off and done something different. And, I might have, if I had not seen the look of sheer joy and expectation on Grandma Penny's face as those opening credits rolled. This was an experience she had been looking forward to for most of her life, and I loved her too much to take that from her.

This movie was black and white, which I was used to. That wasn't a problem for me, even at eight. The strong contrast and practical effects were always more than enough to hold my interest. The very first movie Grandma Penny had watched with me was *The Wizard of Oz*, after all, and the switch from black and white to color is one of the most memorable parts of that movie. True, that one was scary enough in its own way, but since I didn't know of any witches or flying monkeys in my real life, that fear didn't affect me much.

Once the credits ended, I turned my attention away from Grandma Penny's rapt expression back to the movie. The first shot was of the sun, appearing through clouds, with a voiceover:

"In the beginning, God created the heaven and the earth . . ."

And then we were in it.

I was fascinated but wary at the same time. Fires and explosions, and life beginning in the depths. A monstrous hand stretching out of a stone wall and the implication that such creatures had been on the earth for thousands of years. My heart pounded as I watched. Part of me wanted to have these same adventures the scientists had; part of me was glad I was safe at home, on the couch with my grandmother.

So much of the movie—the plot, the characters, the premise—was based on the theory of evolution. When we had gone to the natural history museum, where I had been riveted by the dinosaur skeletons, one of the other exhibits had been about evolution. The basics, of course; only just enough for children to understand the concept. But even at six years old I had gotten it. And now here was a movie explaining to me, perfectly logically even for my eight-year-old mind, how sea creatures could have evolved into humanlike amphibians, and how those same creatures could still be under the surface of the water today.

The particulars of the plot I've now forgotten, but that premise got its hooks in me and has still never let up all these years later.

When the woman seemed to be so carefree, swimming in the lake, all I could think about was all the water around me at any time. Sure, California was in a perpetual drought, but there was the entire West Coast butting up to the Pacific Ocean.

Living in Ventura meant that swimming was a constant, a given. Our proximity to the beach was taken for granted. Starting as early as April, we would head to the beach after school or on weekends. My mom always said that was one of the reasons they paid so much to live where we did, that we should take advantage of the beach as much as possible.

I hadn't even realized how big of a role swimming played in my life up until that point.

One day the previous summer, in the middle of the week when there would be fewer people, Mom had taken off work for the day just for fun. We met up with friends, the Anders family, and both moms, all five kids, and Grandma Penny spent the day in the sun at Ventura Beach. There was a cooler full of sandwiches, another full of drinks, and reminders to reapply sunscreen every few hours.

The Anders kids were all younger than me. Kayla had fun with them, but I usually played with my grandmother or by myself while our moms talked. Just as I was generally allowed to decide for myself if I was ready for something, at the beach I was permitted to go out as far into the ocean as I dared, provided an adult was with me. On this particular visit to the beach, I must have been feeling particularly daring—or maybe I needed attention amongst all those other kids. I pleaded with Grandma Penny to wade out with me.

"Be careful of the undertow," my mom called as Grandma Penny and I strode down the sand to the surf.

"Come on, Grandma!" I called excitedly as I ran.

She jogged to keep up, never once admonishing me to wait for her.

Once we both got in the water, I waded out as far as I could, and once I was chest deep, I continued on, swimming slowly. Every once in a while my feet brushed up against seaweed under the surface, but otherwise I felt only the cold Pacific around me.

"How far do you want to go, Billy?" Grandma Penny asked. "We can't get so tired that we can't swim back."

"I know."

I kept going. I had one eye on the end of the pier. It was maybe half a mile away, of course, but in my mind if I could swim out as far as that it would be an accomplishment worth bragging about.

We kept swimming, so long and so far that Grandma Penny was not able to hide how tired she was getting. Whenever she met my eye she would smile cheerfully, but when she thought I wasn't looking her expression was of such concentration I wonder if she had any other thought than just getting through it.

The things that woman did because she thought it was what I wanted. It's difficult for me to be angry with her even now because of that.

Finally, I had to admit to myself that I was getting tired too. I looked at the pier and told myself I was just as far out as the tip of it. Hard to tell at this distance, but it felt like I was that far out.

"Let's stop here," I said, trying to float on my back even as the waves continued.

Grandma didn't say a thing, just followed my lead. We bobbed there in silence for a minute or so.

I still remember looking down into the dark depths of the ocean and wondering what was under me. We were far enough out that there must be fish or crustaceans scuttling along the ocean floor just yards below my feet.

It had seemed so interesting and magical at the time. There was nothing scary about the mystery; it invited and called to me in an awe-inspiring way that I miss now.

Now, I knew better.

Now, while watching this movie with Grandma, I knew the truth.

There were monsters at the bottom of the ocean, creatures far below me looking up and waiting to grasp my ankles.

The first minute of the movie established the science and the very real—to me—explanation of how such creatures had evolved since the earth came into being. Where a talking scarecrow or someone being mistaken for a spy seemed clearly to be pretend, this monster movie felt just as real as anything else in my life.

I cuddled closer to Grandma Penny, my feet tucked up under me.

As the movie went on, I thought less and less about the fact that it was pretend, and more and more about all the water that I came in contact with every day. We had a neighborhood pool; we went to the beach almost every weekend in the summer. There was even a little creek that ran behind my friend Tony's house that we waded in all the time.

I was in the water far more often than I'd ever realized. Including water in which I could not see the bottom.

Before I even realized it, the movie was over. The good guy had won and the monster had been vanquished. Just as we should have expected.

That's what they wanted me to believe, at least. But all I could think about was where else a monster like that could be hiding. The bottom of the ocean must have millions of places a creature could disappear into, biding their time until the right victim swam above them. Where else might such creatures evolved? How else were such monsters hiding just out of sight?

I could not tear my eyes from the screen, hoping the movie would reassure me somehow, show all the ways that the ocean had been scoured and any other monsters destroyed. I silently pleaded with the film makers to comfort me, to change my mind, to somehow walk back the previous two hours of terror.

My heart beat wildly and my palms sweat as I tried—and failed—to forget the flashes of danger and hidden menace that were now imprinted in my memory. It was all far too believable of a possibility for me to dismiss as fantasy.

"Oh, goodness," Grandma Penny said as the movie ended. "Look at the time. I suppose we don't have time for a bath tonight—we've got to get you to bed."

Chapter 5

Even if Grandma Penny was the cause of my original trauma, it didn't start with her.

Grandma Penny was born Dorothea Ann Lowell, in Burbank, California, in October 1941. She was her parents' first girl and the third of eventually five children.

She was named after her father, my great-grandfather, Ted, who was enamored with his daughter the moment he held her in his arms. In his eyes, she was brilliant, she was beautiful, and she was worth all the stress and abuse he had to put up with at his job to support his family. The two boys born before her—Caleb and Warren—had been wild handfuls, exhausting their mother and constantly getting in trouble for something. Their father only came home from work long enough to sleep and change clothes, though, so what more could be expected? My sister-in-law told me once that being an oldest daughter is a very specific experience of expected maturity well beyond her years; I imagine that's what Grandma Penny went through, especially in the 1940s and '50s. Being given her father's name. Making up for the dashed expectations of the two boys that came before her. At that time it was by no means a given that daughters would go to college or get a job or do anything other than be a wife and mother. That's precisely what she had been raised to be, and what Ted expected of her from the moment she drew her first breath.

After four years of hellions, Ted was convinced parenting a girl would be easier. He promised his wife as much. If I had to guess, I would say that the massive pressure on Dory to be better behaved than her older brothers made any other option unthinkable for her. In all my memories of her, she certainly never let me down or made promises she couldn't keep. Grandma Penny always spoke highly of and with the utmost respect for her father, but the photos I've seen of a serious, clean-cut man in his midcentury suit do not inspire warmth.

Born in Kansas at the beginning of the Great War, Ted Lowell had spent his entire childhood hearing his own father rail against Germany. That country was responsible for so much loss—Ted's uncle died in the war —and destruction. Ted's father was certain that all through the 1920s the Germans were still up to something and had not been thoroughly punished for the disaster they had wrought. When Hitler came to power in 1933, Ted was one of the few Americans who was immediately willing to see the truth of what was happening across the Atlantic and to not be inclined to excuse or sympathize with the rising Nazi party.

He was eighteen and tried to join the Navy immediately, seeing the writing on the wall years before politicians did. They turned him down, due to a slight hearing impairment he'd had since early childhood. But Ted wasn't about to just twiddle his thumbs in the middle of the country, waiting for the opportunity to buy a war bond. His father had settled into farm life well enough after the war, but Ted had bigger plans for himself.

He was a doer, the kind of man who must take action, more often than not in an attempt to control one small part of an otherwise impossible situation.

So instead of being a soldier, Ted somehow got himself a job at Lockheed Martin in Burbank. He had nothing beyond a high school education, but that didn't matter at the time. He kissed his mother goodbye, packed up a single duffle bag of clothes, and made his way to his new life on the coast, where he would work alongside veritable Rosie the Riveters. His five siblings stayed behind in that land-locked state, and I'm not sure Ted ever thought about them again.

Once he had settled in Burbank, Ted lived that midcentury American dream of all middle-class white men: he got married, bought a house, fathered some children, learned to golf, and climbed the corporate ladder, all while ensuring his country had the utmost mechanical support for what was surely to come. Hitler invaded Poland in 1939, the same year that Ted's second child was born. The urgency of making sure the world would be safe for his offspring grew with each news reel out of Europe. He paid attention to each political maneuver and hint coming out of the White House.

All of this meant that when the Japanese bombed Pearl Harbor, Ted Lowell was in a prime position to guide his company to be at the forefront of the war effort when the United States finally entered.

When little Dorothea was two months old.

Although her father stayed stateside all through World War II, she grew up in an environment of war, war, war all the time. Soon, Ted's hard work and determination had been rewarded with more responsibility and requisite pay raises. With as much as the company was expected to produce, and as fast as the president asked for, he was on-call at all times of day. There could be no shirking in the war effort. The horrors of what had happened at Pearl Harbor haunted Ted, and, spurred on by that feeling of helplessness, he grasped for ways to protect his children.

A few months into 1942, Ted learned that one of his classmates from back in Kansas had enlisted and been one of the more than two thousand Americans killed in the attack on Pearl Harbor. As the images of sinking battleships were published, Ted clung to one of the few things he could control.

Namely, it seems, his children.

Specifically, the things his children learned and were exposed to. Ted was determined that even though they were safe in school every day, even though they lived miles from the ocean, his children would not be left to flounder and possibly drown the way many of the soldiers in Hawaii had been. They would never be without that skill that could one day save their lives. The logic was admittedly tenuous, but to this concerned father during the middle of a second world war in his lifetime, it seemed perfectly reasonable a response.

At the time, formal swimming lessons were so rare as to be virtually unheard of. In fact, private swimming pools were reserved for the biggest movie stars. Articles about the enormous swimming pool at Pickfair—the estate shared by film stars Mary Pickford and Douglas Fairbanks —marveled that the ultra-rich could swim in their own backyard in Beverly Hills.

But that didn't stop Ted.

This father's fear that his children could be at the same risk as his friend led him to throw himself headfirst into making sure all of his children could swim and swim well, as young as possible. He started first taking one child at a time to the closest beach, letting them get used to wading, then to standing against the small waves that lapped their ankles, then farther and farther out. By the time Dory was three years old, she was spending all day on the weekends at the beach with her father and brothers, swimming out as far as he would let her, as her mother watched anxiously from the sand.

Once the war was over, once Dory was about four years old and the soldiers came home from overseas, and the government started lining their pockets with GI Bill money, more and more homes in the suburbs were outfitted with private swimming pools. With the war ending, the materials needed for such construction were more plentiful, and every American wanted in on this new era of leisure. Public pools like the Hansen Dam Pool were developed throughout the city, giving the Lowell children more and more opportunities to swim for pleasure, activity, and, most of all, to keep their father from worrying too much about them.

Her older brothers were left alone to roam free like wild animals, and so all the expectations of the family were heaped on Dory, exacerbated when her two younger siblings came along. First Lauren, born when Dory was four, and then baby Timothy a couple years after that.

They, too, were taught to swim as soon as possible, and became just as strong and swift as their older siblings.

Life in the Lowell family was idyllic—until tragedy struck.

When Dory was twelve, her brother Caleb drowned.

Like Dory, Caleb had been given swimming lessons as young as four years old. He was sure in the water, often getting in a swim at the beach in the morning hours before school, and spending all day Saturday at their community pool (whenever he could wheedle his mother into not making him do chores, which was often, the burden of which always went to Dory).

It was that confidence, however, that was his tragic flaw. Since he had been training nearly as long as he had been alive, Caleb thought he knew all there was to know about swimming. He was sixteen and on his high school's swim team. He was being scouted by coaches from all over the country, including a member of the Olympic committee. Nothing had been set or decided, but from what I can tell from family stories passed down over the years, Caleb believed he needed to do something big and flashy to lock down the patronage required to pursue swimming in any professional way. Options for an athlete like him were scant. There were no athletic company sponsorships in 1953. The first athlete did not appear on the front of the Wheaties cereal box until 1958. Caleb would need to be creative to make this a career.

And Ted was cheering his boy on at every step. From the letters that my dad has saved over the decades, it seems like Ted was so certain that Caleb was the consummate athlete that he did not question his son's plan. While their mother may have been more cautious, no one contradicted Ted Lowell.

Caleb's plan was to swim from the beach at Ranchos Palos Verdes across the channel to Catalina Island. It was twenty miles, and though most long-distance swimmers would start at the island and swim to the mainland, due to the tides and the waves making it difficult to leave the shore, Caleb wasn't going to choose the easy option.

Never mind that it had not been done before.

The uniqueness of the feat was half of what attracted Caleb to it in the first place.

I learned later that the first man who successfully swam from the mainland to the island was Jose Cortiñas in October 1953, four months after Caleb's death. Whether Cortiñas knew about the teenager's earlier attempt or not, we may never know.

All the Lowells knew at the time was that, after spending three months training, Caleb had set off bravely and cheerfully early that June morning all by himself. His high school swim coach had chartered a boat to follow alongside him, in the event that anything should happen, but the boy found a way to evade him. With the arrogance and sense of invincibility specific to teenage boys, Caleb had risen a full two hours earlier in the morning than the coach had agreed on, and set off swimming alone just before dawn. By the time the coach realized that Caleb had already started swimming, it was too late to track him down, too late to find him.

Too late to save him.

His body was never recovered.

Dory was with her mother and the two younger children after school when Ted came home to break the news to them. He had taken the day off work; he alone had been privy to Caleb's full plan.

It was a couple years after that when Dory's brother Warren got in trouble for sneaking out to see the monster movie their father had specifically forbidden him seeing. It was a sequel of the movie she eventually showed me, but there's no doubt it would have been just as upsetting. If Ted had been strict and exacting before Caleb died, it was nothing compared to the iron fist with which he ruled his children afterward.

And then, another couple of years after that, Dory married my grandfather, Donald Douglas, who then whisked her north to San Francisco, away from Ted and his expectations.

My father was born less than a year later.

Where Ted had gone above and beyond, insisting his children learn to swim young, pushing them to stay in practice, and even encouraging Caleb's swim team efforts before his accident, Dory went the other way. Without the imperious influence of her father, Dory was better able to create a home of warm acceptance, letting her children take the lead in how they wanted to develop and spend their time. Ted made sure his children had every access to swimming instruction he could possibly provide, while Dory barely said the word *swim* to her children. Though they lived in a neighborhood near a public pool, and only a forty-minute drive from the beach, the Douglases never went. My dad told me he didn't even own swim trunks until he got to high school and was invited to parties with some of his classmates who had backyard pools.

I have often wondered how things might have been different for me if any one of these events had gone differently. If Ted had not lost a friend in Pearl Harbor. If Caleb hadn't taken so well to swimming. If Grandma Penny hadn't settled far from her father's influence.

This timeline is something I pieced together after the fact, once I became an adult. So much of family history is lost not because of trying to keep it secret, but because the younger generations don't ask. I had known that I had a great-uncle that died young, but I didn't know any of the details.

Now, however, I can't help but see the thread running through generations.

The thread—the anchor—that has kept me stuck since I was eight years old.

Chapter 6

That Friday night, cuddled up on the couch next to my beloved Grandma Penny, I didn't know any of that. After a summer full of watching all manner of classic movies, this was the first true monster movie she had shown me. I had been watching the screen intently, as the creature swam up from the depths, as it attacked our heroes, as the mystery of its evolution was explored. I don't know if I even blinked for the entire two hours.

Before that evening, in the fall after I turned eight years old, I had never given the depths of a body of water any thought. Before that strange movie from the 1950s, I hadn't given any thought to any potential evolutionary possibility beyond the animals I already knew about.

But then the movie ended.

The tape stopped. Grandma Penny crossed to the television and turned it off.

"Look at the time," she said. "We've got to get you to bed. I suppose that means no time for a bath."

I froze.

Every other classic movie we had watched together had been fun and exciting. Yes, I had lain awake for a little while thinking about trees getting angry enough to throw their apples, and mops dancing about as they cleaned, but it had never been like this. None of those other stories had ever seemed so close to my own life before this one. Maybe if it had been animated instead of with practical effects, it would have felt more fantastical. Maybe if it had not started with science, if there was more of a mystery around where the creature had come from, it would not have so stayed with me.

Remember, I was eight years old. Remember how your own imagination spiraled when you were that age?

But somehow I had gotten it into my little eight-year-old brain that the creature was real, that something exactly like it was lurking in any body of water big enough or deep enough to hide it. I suddenly remembered feeling the seaweed try to wrap around my feet when we went to the beach.

What if that wasn't seaweed?

It wasn't until Grandma Penny said the word *bath* that I really started to recognize how deeply this film had sunk into my brain. With just that single word, I got a flash of strong, webbed fingers reaching up out of the lake-bottom weeds. I realized I could never again close my eyes in the water. I couldn't hold my breath and be vulnerable like that.

I started breathing heavily, my heart pounding.

"You okay, pumpkin? You must be tired. Come on."

She offered her hand to me, and I clutched for it desperately, like it was a ring buoy.

"Billy? What's wrong?"

But I couldn't tell her. I shook my head and let her lead me to my bedroom.

"It's funny," she was saying. "I wonder why our father didn't want Warren to go see that movie. Although, I suppose now if I think about it, the only movies we were allowed to see were ones Daddy took us to. I should have asked my brother about it."

I was only half listening, wishing it was two hours earlier, before any of those thoughts had entered my mind.

"I'm glad I finally saw it, but I'm not sure I care to watch it again. Do you, Billy? The Disney movies are much more cheerful."

I shook my head, tried to keep my voice steady as I said, "No, thank you."

"Well, there are plenty more films for us to watch." She patted my hand before letting it go so I would walk through my doorway. "Maybe next week we try another of the animated ones. Hurry now, it's late. You know, maybe you should just take a quick bath. It's been a couple days, hasn't it?"

"Please, Grandma Penny." I had turned to face her and clasped at her hand again. "No bath. Not tonight. Please don't make me."

"What has gotten into you?" She frowned. "All right. No bath. It's late anyway. But you're not going to get out of it tomorrow, mister."

She'd promised me I would not have to take a bath that night, and though I could not properly articulate why I was so scared, Grandma Penny did not push me. She sensed that I was agitated, and so she sat with me until my parents got home. They were surprised and disappointed that I was still awake at that time of night, but even they could see that I was frightened, rather than disobedient.

"Must have just been a busy day," Grandma Penny said from my bedroom door when my mom came to tuck me in. "I have trouble sleeping when there's a lot on my mind too."

The following day I still could not succumb to taking a bath without my mind imagining all kinds of sea creatures. And I could not explain my rationale to my parents; the bottom of the tub was right there in clear view. There was nothing hiding, the drain far too small to disguise any manner of danger.

So I compromised. Eight years old, and that is when I started taking showers on my own instead of baths aided by an adult. Mom was wary, but Dad was proud of my independence. I could get in and out quickly enough that I could almost believe I had not gotten fully wet.

I got through that weekend somehow, then the following week, and as it was September, any other reason to be in a body of water would be few and far between. I managed it until I had almost forgotten that I had been so scared in the first place.

That lulling into a feeling of safety, however, is undoubtedly how I ended up triggering my phobia even more strongly the next time.

I had been invited to a pool party the last weekend of the month—my friend Logan's birthday and the last truly hot day of the year. Logan had invited all the kids in our class, even Shelby, who had only transferred to our class in the few days before the party, and Randy, who no one liked. Logan promised that in addition to swimming, his parents had gotten a water slide and set up some kind of waterfall or sprinklers to make the whole pool area like a water park. Rumors abounded, and girls planned matching bathing suits while boys challenged each other to breath-holding contests.

I had been looking forward to the party for weeks. Long enough that I let myself forget about the monster movie, forget about why I had stopped taking baths. Long enough that I could get myself excited about the pool slide and forget what might happen once I got to the end of it.

Grandma Penny took me to the party while my parents stayed home and did Saturday chores. Now that I'm older I see clearly why they must have chosen not to attend an eight-year-old's birthday party, though at the time I secretly thought maybe if they had come they could have kept me safe. Logan lived in our neighborhood, only five blocks away, so with my fresh towel in one hand and his birthday gift in the other, I walked with Grandma Penny to where several other kids were streaming toward the party.

The side gate was open and flanked by balloons, inviting guests to the backyard instead of going through the house. Even though we had timed it so that we arrived at the party right when the invitation said, the swimming and music was still already in full swing before we got there. The smell of hot dogs on the grill made me hungry, and the sight of a wide, frosting-covered sheet cake on a table by the house thrilled me.

I didn't realize it, but I was avoiding looking at the pool.

"You should swim," Grandma said, nudging me a little. She took the birthday gift from me and set it on the card table just inside the side gate. "Give me your towel. I'll look after it until you need it. You go have fun, Billy."

"Will, come on!" Logan called from the top of the water slide.

I took a step toward the pool.

They had in fact set up rows of sprinklers lining the two longer sides of the pool, spraying water in graceful, rainbow-producing arcs into the depths. The tiny ripples of each drop obscured the surface, making anything underwater just that much blurrier.

My stomach felt like lead.

Crystal-clear water, in which I could see all the way to the light blue cement that lined the bottom. Navy and silver tiles ran around the perimeter of the kidney-shaped pool, just under the lip of cement that stretched across the yard. Even though I could see the bottom of the pool, I couldn't trust it. And especially not with the sprinklers making everything more difficult. A flash of memory of the movie from the weekend before reminded me how quickly the monster had coursed through the water, and how slowly I did. I eyed the drain cover in the deep end, thinking that it might just be wide enough across for a body to fit through.

"Go on, Billy. Get some time in before more kids get here and the pool gets too crowded."

I couldn't decide if I would feel more or less safe in the pool when it was filled with twenty other eight-year-olds, but I followed Grandma Penny's instructions.

In a few steps, I was standing at the edge of the pool, my toes curling over the lip.

"You getting in or what?" Randy called from the deep end.

I ignored him.

A couple girls—Sara and Sarah—sat on the second step in the shallow end, their arms linked.

"Excuse me," I mumbled as I walked slowly down the pool steps around them.

The water wasn't as cold as I had feared, and as long as I could feel the steps and cement under my feet, I managed to hold my terror in check. At the bottom of the steps I stood in waist-deep water for a long moment as my body got used to it.

"Will, come dive to the bottom with me!" Logan called. He held a couple neon, weighted batons over his head. "You time me and I'll time you."

But that would mean I would have to go into the deep end. That would mean I would have to go underwater.

There's nothing underwater, I reminded myself. *It's a swimming pool in my friend's backyard, and if I look down I can see all the way to the bottom.*

There's nothing to be afraid of.

I nodded and began to swim to the far end, doggy-paddle with my head above the surface. After a few feet, some of the sprinkler water got in my eye and I had to stop, treading water while I blinked out the stinging.

I felt something brush my ankles, and I kicked out instinctively.

I tried to look around, but all the water in the air made it difficult to know what I was even looking at. More classmates had arrived, and the space was filling with bodies. Willow Evans was close enough that I was afraid of hitting her with my elbow as I tried to tread water.

And amidst all this chaos, a stronger, more insistent

grip on my foot, curiously ticklish on my instep even as the fingers held me in place.

Before I could slip from the grip, it yanked me underwater.

I didn't have a chance to take a breath. My lungs burned with the effort.

I tried to pull away. I tried to reach down and detach the claws from around my foot, but they eluded me. While I was distracted doing that, another hand grabbed my other ankle, holding me under the water more securely.

My bladder let go.

I felt the lower half of my body encased in a cloud of warm liquid that dissipated in the pool far slower than I might have expected.

I kicked. I kicked hard with both feet. Even though I felt sluggish in the water, I threw every single ounce of energy I had into making my legs move hard and fast away from my attacker.

I felt the hands lose their hold.

I kicked hard enough that I hit the cement pool bottom. A spike of pain tore through my foot and I wondered if I had broken a toe. But that, at least, gave me some sense of my surroundings. With nothing else clinging to me, I could finally push off from the bottom of the pool.

When my head finally broke the surface, all around me I heard laughter and shrieking, but it was just a buzz in my ears as I kicked and kicked and flung my arms out to try to get away from what was under the surface. Every swimming lesson I'd ever had left my head. In my frantic effort to get away, I seemed to have spun myself in a circle, no closer to the edge of the pool than before.

I felt fingers on my foot again, but this time I slipped away out of its grip before it could gain any purchase. With my head above water again, I could get my bearings. I was only a couple feet from the edge of the pool now, and I kicked as hard and as fast as I could to close the distance.

I reached out desperately and, first my fingertips, then my whole hand grabbed hold of the lip overhanging the water. With all my upper body strength, I pulled myself out of the pool and onto the hot cement edge, scraping my belly against it. Without looking up, I crawled a foot away, making sure that every single toe was out of the water. I wished I could be dry immediately.

Huddling in the fetal position, I closed my eyes and tried to catch my breath.

Getting out of the pool had helped me come back into myself, but I couldn't completely shake the deep and utter terror that I had felt when my feet had been grabbed under the water.

The sound of my name cut through the noise.

"Will peed!" a boy screamed, cutting himself off with his own laughter. "Will peed in the pool!"

I lifted my head to see Randy Barrett—the class bully who had been held back a year and used his extra height to lord over the rest of us—pointing and laughing at me. He was treading water in the deep end of the pool, a foot or so away from where I had been when I reached the surface.

"Oh, no, Will, were you just so scared?" He mocked

me with a baby-ish voice. "So vewy, vewy scawed you wet your diaper?"

Randy burst into raucous laughter again, deep from his gut, drawing more and more attention from the rest of the class with every breath. Several of the other kids had scrambled to get out of the water upon hearing Randy's accusation. Logan's and a couple of the other parents hurried to the edge of the pool to see what all the fuss was about and to make sure no one had been hurt.

Grandma Penny stayed in the shade of the patio, watching.

Now that I was out of the water, I started to shiver in the September afternoon.

I couldn't look at Randy; I couldn't look at the pool. I was too afraid of seeing the evidence of his words. I could not bear being at this party one more moment.

With my eyes closed, I crawled another couple feet away—so I could further avoid having to look at the site of my humiliation—before getting to my feet. Head hung low, I walked straight to Grandma Penny. She held out a dry towel, ready to wrap me in it, but I took it from her hands and covered my head and shoulders myself. Then I headed for the side gate, past the hot dogs and sheet cake and presents, ignoring the other kids' calls to me, and Grandma Penny followed.

She didn't say a word to me on the walk back home.

I could not stop shaking.

Chapter 7

Logan's birthday party was the last time I went in water deeper than my knees, and to be honest, I don't miss it.

When my family had beach days, I would sit on the sand for hours. I got so sunburnt that first time, but when my mom finally realized I wasn't going to get in the ocean, and since she would not let me stay home, she bought an umbrella for me to sit under. I flat-out refused to even attend any pool parties over the years, to the point that by my sophomore year I was no longer invited. Instead, I filled my time with math and chess, two activities that would never even take me outdoors.

I won't pretend it was easy. I made other friends, of course. Logan never pressured me to swim when we hung out at his house, and there are plenty of things to do other than swimming—bowling birthday parties and sleepovers and touch football. But remember, this was Ventura. The beach was just steps away and the promise of swimming pools was constant. My entire childhood from eight-years-old onward was lonely and embarrassing just because of this one little thing; I had to either explain over and over again why I didn't want to get in the water, or come up with some other reasonable explanation.

As for Grandma Penny, after we left Logan's she must have realized how much that movie had scared me. Our walk home was silent, but once we reached our front door, she stopped me before I could go in, her hand a light pressure on my shoulder.

"Billy," she said softly. "Do you want to tell me what happened back there? Did you hurt yourself, or . . . ?"

But I didn't know how to respond. I was just a kid, with a wild imagination and any number of illogical defenses for how I felt. I thought I would be in trouble if I told her the truth, that it was my fault that I couldn't put those scary images out of my mind. As Grandma Penny looked down at me with concern on her face, I was absolutely certain that if I said any of what I was feeling out loud, it would be the end of everything.

"Yeah, I kicked the bottom of the pool on accident," I mumbled. The toes on my right foot were a bit pink and possibly swollen, if you looked hard for it. "I just want to be home. I should maybe rest my feet or something."

She nodded, though her gaze continued to probe me. "All right, then. I'll take a look."

"That's okay," I said over my shoulder as I opened the front door and limped inside. "I'll get Mom to do it."

I didn't look back to see how she was taking the rejection.

At that moment, I didn't much care.

I spent the rest of the day in my room, with ice on my toes long past when the pain had subsided. But staying off my feet was a good excuse to avoid Grandma Penny that day, the injury itself a good excuse for coming home from the party early.

I came up with different tactics after that.

That was decades ago. I will never know for certain what she guessed or found out. She probably did her best to undo what she had done—suggesting different movies, and then different hobbies altogether that we could do together. But the damage had been done. All I really remember is the overwhelming anxiety each time she tried to show me some new film. My eight-year-old heart had been betrayed and I could not trust her. I couldn't be sure that the same thing might not happen again.

The next few years, I avoided Grandma Penny as much as I possibly could. I threw temper tantrums and made up lies and pretended to be sick, rather than be alone with her at all. I refused to watch any movie that was older than I was, and I mocked the ones that I saw Grandma watching without me. I was young and heartless and frankly kind of a jerk to this woman who had given up her own life to come help raise her grandchildren. But I just wanted to put as much distance between us as I could.

As Kayla got older, and as I grew even pricklier, Grandma Penny directed her energy toward my sister instead. There were occasional invites and overtures in my direction, but I rebuffed every single one. Kayla did not appear to suffer anything close to what had scarred me; she was never interested in watching the classic movies, but even beyond that her growing up was far different than mine. I still don't truly understand how siblings can have such dissimilar experiences despite being in virtually the same environment.

Partly because of my fear, partly because of good old teenage rebellion, but also partly because of Grandma Penny, when the time came I decided I wanted to go away to college. Another state if possible. My parents weren't thrilled about it—I was reminded at least ten times how less expensive the state schools would be if I remained a California resident. But I could be stubborn. Nothing was going to change my mind. I wanted to live somewhere on my own, somewhere I could start fresh and put all of this behind me. I wanted to make new friends and not be surrounded by the same classmates who had seen my utter breakdown so many years before.

So I chose to attend Arizona State University, sight unseen. It wasn't all that hard to get into and was large enough that any major I decided on would be accessible. Mostly, though, that school was deliberately chosen because of the dearth of water in Phoenix. As I had never visited the state until moving into my dorm that hot August week, however, I had no idea how many homes in that city came with swimming pools. Every apartment complex or even neighborhood with a community center sported a pool—essential for cooling off in those desert summers. There may even be more areas to swim in the greater Phoenix area than in my hometown.

There was no escaping it.

I spent another several years being miserable, blaming my grandmother and lashing out my anger at other people.

I know better now. As an adult I can see that none of this was Grandma Penny's fault. She had wanted to share with me something she thought I would like. She was actively making an effort to find things for us to do together. I have friends who would have killed to have a grandparent in their life like that. If only things could have been different for me. If it had been a couple years later I probably would have been able to better appreciate the make-believe element of the movie. Or maybe I wouldn't have felt as though I had to respond to the pressure from Grandma Penny at Logan's.

To be honest . . . I don't know.

I'm less angry now, but no more healed. I'm not an expert. I'm just a man who has had to spend years struggling to cope with what is perfectly normal to millions of others.

There's no telling what seeds one person's trauma but not others'. There's little way to predict what unexpected thing will trigger big emotions. All I did was watch a movie from the 1950s. It scarred me deeply. It poisoned my relationship with my favorite person and made me irrationally afraid of water.

That series of choices and attitudes all culminated to change my life irrevocably. From one generation to another, each step along the way has brought me to this point. I could not have avoided it, even if I knew it was coming.

I'm embarrassed to admit it now, but I never made up with Grandma Penny.

When I was nineteen, she died. I had moved away from home the year before and had not bothered to come back for the holidays. I told myself there was time, that this was my first Christmas on my own, that home would always be there for me.

Kayla called to tell me, scolding me more vehemently than our parents would ever dare. I returned home for the funeral, but it did not feel like a real goodbye. Not when there were so many things left unsaid between us.

And that new layer of regret piled on only made everything that much harder.

In spite of my fresh start, I had a hard time making friends in Arizona. With so much of social life based around people's backyard pools, there was only so many times a person would extend to me an invitation before they gave up. I tried, half-heartedly, but ultimately decided to transfer to a different school. My senior year, and then grad school, was spent at Colorado University, Boulder. Of course there are lakes and rivers and even some pools there, but there was also so much else to do that I could avoid them far more easily. I taught myself to snowboard instead, got a dog, went for long hikes in the mountains.

I thought I had it figured out. I thought I was doing so well, in fact, that I began to really regret not patching things up with Grandma Penny before she died. I found a career that I enjoyed and made friends and was able to forget my phobia for weeks at a time. Finally—finally—everything was falling into place.

And then I met Robyn.

At the time I lived a mile and a half away from campus and rode my bike most days. On particularly sunny days I gave myself extra time so I could cool down before class in the air-conditioned library. One September afternoon, halfway through my MBA program, when I stepped into the library, the first thing I saw was this young woman, honey-blond hair piled in a knot on the top of her head. She wore glasses that kept slipping down her nose and was so engrossed in the textbook open in front of her—*Introduction to Chemical Engineering Thermody- namics*—that I was able to watch her push her glasses back up no fewer than five times.

I noticed her drink was almost empty, so I found a vending machine, bought her a bottle of water, and intro- duced myself.

Within eighteen months we got engaged, moved in together, and got married on the side of a mountain with our family and friends surrounding us. We made plans for our future together and settled into a peaceful life side by side. Robyn had heard some of my issues with water—I absolutely refused to go on a cruise for our honeymoon— but I never felt like it was necessary to give her all the gory details.

Through our courtship, Robyn had mentioned wanting to have children "one day." Most girls I had dated said something like that, and I stupidly thought the "one day" being in the future would give me time to come around to wanting them, too, or give her time to change her mind.

Neither thing has happened.

In fact, it seems as though both Robyn and I have become more committed to our choices. I deflected well, rationalizing that not answering a direct question is still an answer. About two years ago, Robyn became more persistent. She has been asking me every single month when she fills her birth control prescription if I am still unsure.

That's when I had to start lying to her outright. Every time I thought about helping a little boy learn to ride his bike, I had a minor panic attack realizing I would have to help him learn to swim too. Every time I thought about the absolute unreality of the movie that actually scared me, I worried about what other ostensibly harmless thing could be lodged in a child's imagination.

I had had too difficult a time with all of this to risk passing it on to another generation. Not that I was ready to tell Robyn that.

And that's where we stood until twenty-five days ago.

I had successfully convinced myself that I had everything under control until one seemingly innocuous house-warming party.

Chapter 8

Twenty-five days ago, my fear was again brought to the surface, and I could not pretend anymore.

After the reminder of how badly I was affected by my fear, I realized I could not lie to Robyn anymore. After six years, and another week of arguing, I finally told her plainly that I was serious about not having kids. I haven't been clear before, but now I am putting my foot down. This is not negotiable. We had only discussed it cursorily in the past, leaving the possibility open, waiting for the right timing or the sign that it should be our next step.

But now I've told her the truth; now she knows that I have been deceiving her since we met.

That house-warming party . . .

Even now, I don't understand how I once again found myself in the same vulnerable situation. Though I had never let down my guard around water since that day when I was eight years old, I had so successfully distanced myself from the child I was that the people in my life now have no idea of the depth of my phobia. I don't need to be coddled. I can take care of myself. But at the same time, if I am the only person who understands exactly the risk I would be taking by, say, wading in a river, any excuses I try to make don't sound serious.

Setting boundaries with other people is exhausting. And I had convinced myself it would just be easier to go along with what my wife and friends wanted.

It seems like I keep trying. And I keep failing.

Something has to change, something beyond Robyn not speaking to me.

Twenty-five days ago, Robyn and I were invited to a house-warming party for friends who finally—after years of saving, a little help from their parents, and the crash of the housing market—were able to buy their first home. Very suburban, very cookie-cutter. A starter home in almost every way, but Jason and Mitch were excited. They had been looking forward to this for so long, longer than the seven years I've known them. Of course we would go cheer them on. I did not give a second thought to being there to support them and celebrate. Robyn bought a fancy bottle of wine and a cheese tray, and that Sunday afternoon we drove across town to the party.

It is a newer house, built in a planned community that sat empty for the beginning of the recession. They got a good deal on it. In true Colorado fashion, the environment surrounding civilization is given top priority. There's no golf course to suck up the water resources, and the streetlights are designed to put out as little light pollution as possible. The neighborhood is built around the natural landscape, with the placement of the house lots and roads accounting for the root systems of old trees and—to my dismay—the paths of creeks and rivers.

I don't know if they just never mentioned this fact or if I had somehow blocked it out, but Jason and Mitch's backyard butts up against a wide, shallow creek that serves as their property boundary. They're very excited about that feature, to say the least, convinced that they'll walk out to drink their coffee with the frogs every morning.

As a good friend, I smiled and nodded, encouraging their excitement, even as inwardly I began to panic. Robyn and I live in a second-floor apartment, with a view of the mountains. Far, far away from any body of water.

"There's no one living in the house behind us yet," Jason was saying as he led our small group across the backyard. "We've only been here a few weeks, but having our own little creek has been so much more relaxing than I ever would have guessed."

"I told him he should name it," Mitch teased, winking at his partner. "Like a proper man of leisure overseeing his estate."

"You'd better watch it, or I'll do that very thing."

We kept walking, but I started to trail behind the others. The closer we got to the creek the faster any excuses I wanted to make simply flew from my mind. I could see in my wife's face that she would be just as excited as Jason if we were to ever have a home with our own creek.

"I'll show you here where we cross," Mitch was saying. "It's pretty easy. And then we'll cut through this other yard so you can see the dog park. It's about half a mile away if we were to walk on the sidewalks, but as long as there's no one to stop us we've been going this way."

Still, I hung back. Crossing that thing? Maybe—

maybe—if there was a proper footbridge I could do it without panicking, but like this? I shook my head, though no one was paying attention to me; no one would have recognized that as a refusal.

Mitch, at least, told the truth: it did look easy.

We reached the edge of the creek, where it was about eight feet across. Wider than other stretches, but the bigger stones that were scattered in the water offered a far more apparent path.

"How deep is it?" I asked, trying to keep the shake from my voice.

"I don't know." Mitch frowned and looked and Jason. "What do you think, babe?"

Jason looked at the water and then back at me. "Maybe knee-deep? Maybe a little bit more?"

I nodded. It didn't matter. Even water in which I could see the bottom was too deep for me.

But what were my choices? I had spent my entire time in Colorado avoiding having to explain any part of this paranoia. Was I supposed to start now? Make a big deal during this celebration for my friends?

Regardless, the question of where politeness and consideration of others fits in coping with a person's trauma and mental health issues is moot. It's obviously something I should have considered before we ever left the house.

Because in that moment, all I could think about was not wanting to make my hosts feel bad, but more than that not giving my wife any reason to worry about me. How would she look at me differently if she knew I was so against crossing a few feet of knee-deep water where (probably) nothing could hurt me?

Mitch crossed blithely, practically dancing in his little leaps across the gaps from one stone to another. Their friends Kaye and Lisa went next, with Jason crossing soon after.

"Ready?" Robyn said to me as she started her own way across.

I stood a full foot away from the riverbank and eyed the water bubbling past. If it was slightly more narrow I might have attempted to leap over it.

Robyn had made her way to the third flat stone, about halfway across the creek.

"Come on, Will," she insisted, holding out her hand for me to take. "Just a couple steps."

It was now or never. Was I going to try to put my fear aside so my wife doesn't have to worry about me or be embarrassed by me, or was I going to make up some lie, go back to the house by myself, and further build up the walls around me that have been there for decades?

I nodded, stepped closer to the edge.

"Careful," Robyn called unnecessarily.

Just a few steps, and then it would be over. I could insist that after the dog park they take us back through the neighborhood. So we could see all aspects. Right?

Sure.

But first I had to get through the most harrowing situation I had put myself in in years—and that's counting the six months I struggled to learn how to snowboard.

With the smallest jump, I took a long step to the first stone. I held my balance. My heart started beating more fervently, as though wanting to fit in as much life as possible in these last few moments before I perished.

"You got it?" Robyn asked. Then she turned her back

to me and took the final few steps to the other side of the creek, where everyone else was waiting.

And watching me.

I kept my eyes on my feet. I thought if I looked up, looked around, even for a split second, I would remember exactly the risks I was taking.

One more short step.

And that was as far as I got.

My balance was off; my shoes got wet. I placed my sneaker down with all my weight and knew it was a mistake. My foot slipped on a mossy stone. I yelped as I felt the loss of control, as my foot touched the creek bottom—mud, more rocks, moss, weeds, and I can only imagine what else. All those creatures I could not see that lurked at the bottom of bodies of water.

And I stepped right into it.

As my foot slipped, I lost my balance, arms pinwheeling, and fell back onto my butt into the water. It came halfway up my chest as the slow currents wove around me. My frightened yelp turned into a sob as I felt so much of my body underwater. In cloudy water. I had bruised the palms of my hands as well as the back of my right thigh in the fall onto the stones lining the bottom of the creek. I could not see my hands even as I had to push myself against one of the stones to bring myself to a standing position.

"Will?" Robyn called, a note of concern in her voice as she watched me crying and stumbling in a creek that wouldn't scare a toddler. "Will, did you hurt yourself?"

Jason hurried to my side, his own shoes getting drenched in the process as he helped me to my feet. The house-side of the creek was closer, and he guided me toward the building.

"We'll get these shoes off him. You all go along. We'll be fine."

I let myself be taken care of, grateful that my wife was spared the full extent of my sobbing. It was clear Jason didn't know exactly what to say to me; it was clear that I was upset by something far deeper than a bruised ego.

In twenty minutes he had gotten me dried off, in clean comfy clothes, and curled up on their couch with a couple fingers of bourbon.

"You, uh . . . you're okay?" he said finally, after I had sat silently for ten minutes. "They'll probably be back soon. Do you need anything?"

Left unsaid was the fact that my wife had not followed herself to make sure I was okay. Left unsaid was the absolutely irrational sobbing from a grown man after he had gotten his attire a little bit wet.

I shook my head, thanked him, and promised to bring his clothes back to him clean.

The front door opened and Mitch led the others back into the house. Robyn wasn't looking at me, but I stood and thanked our hosts.

"Want me to call a cab?" I asked Robyn. "I'm going home, but you can stay."

She answered lightly, no hint of the emotion that she was holding back, and we left together with my wife driving. There was no conversation on the drive, but as soon as we walked in our apartment door, Robyn confronted me.

"You're keeping something from me, Will. What was that? What was all that? You can't do that to me. We're supposed to be partners, and I can't . . . it's not a partnership if you are not being yourself. Tell me what's going on. Please."

But where do I start?

I gave her the short version—childhood fear, coping mechanisms I've developed—and promised I would speak up in the future if we were in a similar situation.

That was twenty-five days ago. Twenty-four days ago, I had a panic attack in the shower. Then I found other ways to keep clean while I tried to placate Robyn. At first she was confused, concerned. She wanted to know how she could help. And then, when it became clear that this fear of mine stretched well beyond not wanting to go swimming, she seemed angry.

Those conversations were circular, where I tried in numerous ways to explain the same thing in different words, until finally I let slip the one thing that had been growing more and more certain since we left Jason and Mitch's.

"This is why I don't trust myself with kids," I said, exasperated after another two hours of pointing out all the ways this fear had run my life. "Why I left California, and Phoenix, and why I never want to go to any of these community festivals you keep putting on the calendar."

She frowned. "What does any of that have to do with kids?"

That was eighteen days ago. She spent two more days trying to understand, trying to talk about it, trying to get me to backtrack and change my mind, trying to make me see how much my deception had hurt her.

All fair. All valid.

All useless.

And then she just stopped talking to me altogether.

I took my recent setback as the sign that it is not the right step, that having kids would be the worst thing that we could perpetuate upon this earth. Generations of parents making the best choices they knew to make for their children has still ended up with billions of traumatized, unstable, anxious, uncertain adults. I am no better than my great-grandfather was, and I have no doubt that I would screw up my own children as much as he did.

And his father before him.

And on and on.

I've spent twenty-one years of my life dealing with this.

Before I even met Robyn, I had the vague idea that I should not inflict anyone else with what had so scarred me.

I made this decision not to be a father years ago. It is deep in my bones and unwavering.

My wife does not appreciate me making that decision for us.

She hasn't spoken to me in sixteen days.

But she has communicated.

This afternoon I was served with divorce papers. When I got home from work, her side of the closet had been cleaned out. There was no note, but I think my texts are still being delivered, so at least she has not blocked me entirely.

I don't know what happens next, but whatever it is, I only have myself to blame for how I've handled all this. For thinking I could just fake my way around such a strong fear, for thinking that my partner did not need to know this huge part of my life.

I find myself actually looking forward to my therapy appointment. I still have hope this fear is not so deep in me that it cannot be exorcised. I have to have hope of that. Even if I am alone throughout the process. I haven't signed the divorce papers; Robyn has not yet agreed to dinner with me but she hasn't turned me down either.

And who knows? Maybe the thread doesn't have to be cut. Maybe, like a newly formed river, it can forge a new path.

Free Stories!

Sign-up at AmyTeegan.com/free for two free short stories, updates and reading recommendations.

Author's Note

Thank you so much for reading this sad and dark novella. The story originally was intended to be a fraction of the length and included in my 2020 short story collection *POISON*, but it kept growing. I decided it needed to stand on its own.

Just so we're clear, this story doesn't resemble anything in my own life or family. When I first announced the publication, my mother commented on the Facebook post: "family? Should we be worried?"

No, Mom. All of my grandparents were delightful and none of them scarred me in any way that I am aware of. While, like most people with large families, I *do* have relatives that died in tragic circumstances, none of them were by drowning. The theme of unintentional generational trauma seems so universal that I honestly don't remember where specifically I got the idea for this story. I believe it mostly stemmed from the idea of something seemingly innocuous affecting your life in a disproportionate way.

Some things that I did steal from my real life:

When I was in elementary school, my grandma Jay came to live with us for a few years, but that's where the similarity ends. She cooked and cleaned and walked me to school. She read romance novels and watched The Price is Right. She's the reason I crave chicken and dumplings now and then. I miss her.

I did grow up in Southern California and while we did not have a swimming pool, plenty of my friends did. I went to pool parties when I was a kid, and my best friend who lived on our street had one. I have no specific memory of learning to swim, because it was just always part of my life. In fact, the earliest memory I have is of playing in the kids' wading pool at the community pool in Tempe, Arizona, when I was maybe three years old.

Anndddd… I think that's it.

I love history in general, and the shiny facade of mid-20th century Hollywood and post-WW2 culture hiding what's underneath in particular. It's a theme of many of my books and stories. So, as you can imagine, I did far more research for this short novella than a person might expect. I love the context, though, and I love the details. I found quite a few historic photos of public pools, as well as more general cultural discussions of what those communal spaces mean.

I would read an entire in-depth non-fiction book on swimming in early twentieth century Southern California if such a thing existed (let me know if you find one).

In the meantime, I've collected the half-dozen links to articles from around the web here:

https://amyteegan.com/deep-research/

Enjoy!

Though it is never explicitly named in the text, the old movie that Grandma Penny shows Will is *Creature from the Black Lagoon*. I watched it for the first time when I was dreaming up this story, and I firmly believe that a lot of the practical special effects used in movies from the mid-20th century were too real and particularly traumatizing to small children. I imagine there are adults everywhere who remember being scared of the attacking trees from *Wizard of Oz,* or the dinosaurs in *King Kong*.

Special thanks as always to Spencer Hamilton—my best friend who lets me talk his ear off about story ideas and character moments and random research, and my editor who makes my prose tight and flawless before publishing. Every single thing I write would be not quite as good if he wasn't in my life.

Thanks to OneMind, my small mastermind of indie authors that I have been meeting with regularly since … 2015? 2016? I honestly don't remember. A really long time. They all know me and know my business and know my brain better than any co-worker I have ever had. My career would look a lot different without the regular support and advice from Alyssa, Claire, Hayley, Kerry, Monica and Kalvin.

Thanks to what I lovingly refer to as 'my scrapbooking ladies' even though I personally have not been involved in scrapbooking for years. Kam, Kristin and Megan are always there to cheer me on and support whatever my new project is. I'm pretty sure one of them was the first to preorder this book.

Thanks to Gerry for guiding me through making the changes in my business necessary so I could get off the pen-name-pulpy-hamster-wheel and have the time to write this book at all.

Thanks to my parents (and other family) who did not scar me in any particularly destructive way. Thank you for giving me so many years in Southern California because I will be using that backdrop for books for years to come.

And thanks to you, my reader, for giving this novella a shot. I know better than most that this genre takes some discerning, brave readers to try out stories that don't fit into the common, best-selling categories. Thank you for giving me a chance to write what I love.

About the Author

Amy Teegan is a reader, writer and traveler currently living in central Pennsylvania.

Follow her at amyteegan.com.

Also by Amy Teegan

No Day Like Today

Poison: Stories

9 781949 153279